The breakup

Kayla shouted dinner is ready. Kara and I ran downstairs as quickly as we could to see who would get there first. I won this time. Kayla just laughs every time we compete to see who gets to the dinner table first.

Kayla gave us our pasta dinner. We were eating when Kara, my white sister said Kevin and I broke up. I said oh no Kara I'm sorry about that and Kayla my white mommy said oh my god that bastard and right before prom when you've already gotten your dress.

Kara said I know and now I have no date to the prom. I said I can be your date to the prom if you don't mind. Kara said you would do that for me. I said of course I'm happy to do that for you. We hugged and kissed with Kara saying thank you so much I owe you big time for this one.

Kayla hugged and kissed me saying that is very sweet of you to do this for Kara. I said my pleasure. Kayla said you have your tuxedo, so we are all set, I can't wait to take pictures of the most adorable couple at the prom. We both giggled at Kayla when she said that to us.

After we finished dinner, Kayla was clearing the plates and I smacked her juicy big ass and said thanks for dinner. She said you're welcome honey and Kara giggled. Kara thinks it's funny every time I smack her mother's sexy big ass.

Kayla loves her ass smacked so I do it all the time now. Kara and I went to our rooms. I went to Kara's room and hugged her tight. I said sorry about Kevin. She said its ok and thanks for being my date to the prom. I said my pleasure and I kissed her rubbing her back.

Kara leaned on me, and I held her for a long time as we talked. We watched television cuddled up. Kayla came in and said I was wondering where you were. I said just here consoling Kara. I wiped the tears from her pretty face. Kayla said don't cry my love and she started crying too.

All three of us were in the bed hugging and having a good cry as a family. Kayla is a great single white mommy raising two seniors after the divorce from Kent. I said we should all sleep here tonight, Kara and Kayla agreed with me. So, we all got ready for bed. I had on my boxers only while

Kayla and Kara wore big t-shirts to bed showing off their sweet white thighs.

We all cuddled up in Kara's king size bed and drifted off to sleep. My alarm on my apple smart watch went off. It was time to get up. I said wake up sleeping beauties. It's time for work and school. Kayla said I'll go make us breakfast and Kara went to her bathroom. I went to my bathroom to get ready too.

We ate breakfast together as we normally do every day. When we finished Kara and I went to our prep school while Kayla went to her law firm. I smacked Kayla's ass for good luck at work today before she left, and Kara giggled.

Prom night, I put on my tuxedo while Kayla helped Kara get ready. When Kara came out wow. I said you are going to be the most beautiful girl at this prom. She gave me a wonderful smile and she said you look very handsome too.

Kayla said both of you look incredible now let's get as many pictures as possible before the

*limousine arrives. Kayla had her camera ready on
a tripod. She started taking pictures of Kara and
me. We did the poses that she wanted and then she
said I need one with a kiss. We kissed and Kayla
got the picture. Kayla took pictures first with both
of us then separately. I got a picture of me
smacking her juicy ass and kissing her too.*

*The three of us heard the limousine horn beep and
the picture session was over. Kayla said have a
great time at the prom, I love you both very much.
We said we love you too. We held hands and
walked to the Limousine, I helped Kara wearing
an amazing pink evening gown into the Limousine
and then I climbed in.*

*We held hands all the way to the prom. When we
arrived, I got out and helped Kara out of the
Limousine. She looked so hot; I couldn't wait to
dance all night with her. We walked in and said
our hellos to our school mates and teachers.*

*Kara and I started dancing while smiling the
whole time. When Kara saw Kevin with his date,
she held me tighter and grind her vagina into my
penis. I had a full-blown erection in sixty seconds*

of her doing that and I said oops sorry about that Kara. She said don't be, your big penis feels really good on my vagina. Later she moaned and said you're making me super wet with that big thing. I said both of us are feeling really good. Kara laughed out loud. Kevin gave me the stink eye when I made Kara laugh. I told Kara and she said fuck him. I laughed out loud.

After dancing for a while, Kara said I need to rest before I can't walk home. I said sure no problem. We sat down and were talking when Miss Heather came over to us. We both said hi Miss Heather, she asked Kara if she could dance with me. Kara said sure knowing that I had a crush on Miss Heather ever since 9th grade. Miss Heather is really pretty and had amazing Texas curves.

I said I would be honored to dance with you Miss Heather. I never missed an English class of Miss Heather in 4 years of high school. We held each other close and danced. She put her head on my shoulders and rubbed my arms. Oh my god that really turned me on to a full-blown erection.

*I said I'm so sorry Miss Heather. She surprised
me by saying your 18 now anything goes plus I
really like you and I'm wet. I said Miss Heather
I've been in love with you since the 9th grade. Miss
Heather said I know honey from the way you have
looked at me over the years. Miss Heather said
after you graduate, you should come to my house
for a visit, I live alone. I said I would love to visit
you, Miss Heather. I gave her my number and she
texted me her address.*

*We grind on each other for a while smiling, she
said we better stop before I kiss you. I said yeah, I
better get back to my date. I went back to Kara,
and she was smiling. I said what are you smiling
about, Kara said I know you love her, and you
probably got hard dancing with her.*

*I said I do love her, and I did get hard dancing
with her. She told me that I made her wet. Kara
said wow you made two white vaginas wet tonight.
I said it's a very good prom night. The music
stopped and we all headed for the exit. Miss
Heather hugged me goodbye and said thanks for
the dance. I said you're welcome, Miss Heather.*

Kara and I left to go home. Kayla was waiting up for us. She asked, how was the prom. I said great and Kara said he danced with Miss Heather. Kayla said the one he is in love with, Kara said oh yeah. Kayla hugged me tight and said that is great honey.   I kissed Kayla and smacked her ass, I said thanks sweet cheeks. Kara giggled and we all went to bed.

I laid in my bed horny and hard. Kara text me that she can't sleep. I said I'm too horny to sleep. Kara replied me too, do you want to stick that big thing in me and get rid of our horniness. I said are you serious. Kara sent me a picture of her wet white pussy and I replied with a picture of my hard-black cock leaking precum. Kara replied get over here you big dick stud.

I ran over to her room and Kara was naked in the middle of her bed smiling. I was completely naked too, I jumped on her kissing her like crazy. Kara said please stick it in baby I'm so wet. I pushed and pushed until I was able to force my black dick into Kara's white pussy.

*I said oh wow I'm finally in and Kara said it feels
so good. I started fucking her pussy and she
moaned I really need this tonight thanks for
coming to my room to fuck me. I said my pleasure
as I gave it to her good. She held me tight as we
fucked for a long time. Kara squeezed me tight
every time she came, and her head went
backwards. When my eyes rolled back in my head,
and I said oh god. Kara said oh yeah stud come in
your white sister. I held Kara tightly and said
thanks for the white pussy and she said thanks for
the big black cock.*

*I said I feel so much better now as we laid side by
side. Kara said same here, I haven't had cock
since I broke up with my boyfriend. I said my
pleasure sexy Kara, she said you're welcome my
black stud. We hugged and kissed goodnight.*

*I was walking to the door naked when Kara said
you look great naked. I said thanks Kara, so do
you and she smile at me. I closed her door and
walked to my bedroom. I was too steps away from
my bedroom when Kayla appear totally naked.*

I said oh my god, you are the sexiest woman in the world. Kayla said thanks, why are you naked. I said oh no I'm getting a boner. Kayla looked down and saw my hard cock, she said wow that's big. She said why is there cream on your big black cock.

I said its Kara's we had sexual intercourse and now I'm trying to sneak back to my room before my hot white mommy catches me. Kayla laughed and said thanks for telling me the truth. I said the truth will set you free and you know I need to smack that ass while you're naked.

Kayla said I know, she turned around, and I said you have the most perfect ass. I smacked her ass and she moaned, then I smacked the other cheek and she moaned again. Kayla turned and kissed me. I grabbed her big booty then we started making out like crazy. My hard cock slid between her sweet white thighs to rub on her pussy.

I felt wetness from her pussy. I stopped our kiss and said how come your wet. Kayla said you smacking my ass makes me wet every time. I said oh really. I kissed her again and we fell against

*the wall. Kayla jumped on my hips I held her
sweet white thighs and slid her down my black
pole.*

*Kayla moaned oh God your big cock is so deep in
my white pussy fuck me my black son. I haven't
had cock since the divorce. I started pumping my
black cock deep in and out of her white pussy. I
moaned because it felt so fucking good, and Kayla
moaned with pleasure too. I kept hammering her
pussy for a while then Kayla held me tight, and I
felt her cream on my cock and balls. I put her
down and I told her to assume the position.*

*Kayla bent over and held on the railing. I
smacked her ass cheeks again before I penetrated
her white pussy again. I held her hips and went to
town on her pussy. Both of us were biting our lips
and moaning as we enjoyed the fuck. I said damn
Kayla you have some good ass pussy here baby.*

*Kayla said thank you honey, and you have the best
dick ever. My orgasm hit me, and I held her hips
firm and unloaded all the sperm I had in my balls
into hot Kayla. I moaned oh god so good. Kayla*

said thank you baby for satisfying your white mommy's horny pussy.

We hugged and kissed good night. I squeezed her big booty and said best ass in Texas. Kayla had the biggest smile on her pretty face. I watched her jiggle away and she looked back at me before I went into my bedroom to sleep.

The next morning at breakfast. We were eating with a lot of sexual tension in the air. Kara said mom I had sexual intercourse with my black brother last night after prom. We were both still horny, I summoned him to my room, we had great sex and I loved every second of it. I said it was great sex, I loved it too.

Kayla said that's great honey thanks for telling me and I'm not mad at either of you. She said I caught your black brother sneaking back to his bedroom naked after he fucked you. We had sexual intercourse too on the wall, then he bent me over the railing and took us both to heaven.

Kara was shocked then looked at me and said someone had a great prom night. I said I guess all three of us had a great prom night. All three of us were smiling then Kara said wow his sperm is in both of us. It blew my mind when she said it, Kayla said I was extra turned on with him sticking his dick in me after he took it out of your pussy.

Kara said oh my god that is so kinky and erotic. When we finished our breakfast. I lifted up Kayla's robe and smacked her bare ass. She moaned and Kara giggled then she asked her mom does that turn you on when he smacks your big ass. Kayla said it gets me wet every time. Kara said oh wow then she looked at me and said can you smack my fat ass too. I want to see if it works on me too.

I said ok, she bent over and lifted up her robe. I smacked her bare ass and she moaned too. Kara said oh yeah that works on me too. Kayla said like mother like daughter. We all laughed out loud.

Graduation day came up quickly before we could blink after prom. Kayla was smiling the whole day. She told us how proud that she was for both

*of us to be graduating. We both said thank you
and when we were ready in our cap and gowns.*

*Kayla took pictures then started crying which
made us all cry. We regained our composure then
finished taking all the pictures that Kayla needed.
We drove to the graduation ceremony in silence as
we all took in this momentous occasion. Soon we
would be graduating then off to college.*

*Kara was wearing just panties and bra under her
graduation gown. I was wearing just boxers so we
would not be too hot in the oppressive Texas heat.
Kara and I were sitting next to each other. We
listened to all the speeches then it was time to get
our diplomas. Kara was first then I followed her
closely watching her ass jiggling in her gown.*

*I was happy that I wore a gown because I was
hard. Kara collected her diploma and then it was
my turn to collect my diploma. I collected it shook
principal Megan's hand then I saw Miss Heather
put out her arms for a hug. I was panicked
because it had a boner then I realized that she has
felt my boner before then I hugged her tight.*

*Miss Heather said congratulations to my favorite
student. I said thank you Miss Heather, I love
hugging you and she said it's always a pleasure
hugging you baby. I let hot Miss Heather go and
followed Kara back to our seats. Kara asked if I
hugged Miss Heather. I said yeah and I had a
boner thanks to looking at your sexy ass jiggling in
front of me. Kara said you're welcome lover.*

*I said good thing principal Megan didn't try to hug
me too or there would have been an incident of her
eyes popping out of her head. The religious nut is
hot but uptight as hell. Kara laughed out loud
then said very true.*

*After our class got our diploma, we met up with
Kayla in a tight sexy summer dress. She hugged
and kissed both of us, congratulating us and telling
us that she is the proudest mommy ever. We both
said thank you and we thanked her for 4 years of
hard work getting us through high school in one
piece.*

*Kayla said you're welcome now let me get some
pictures. We took pictures galore then said our
goodbyes to our friends and teachers. Kara and I*

*were off for the summer. Kayla took us to a
graduation dinner. We talked like normal and ate
as other people around us stared at the black guy
with the two hot white ladies.*

*Saturday morning, I texted Miss Heather asking
her when it is a good time to come over since I just
graduated. She said how about 8 pm tonight. I
said sure, I'll be there. I told Kara and Kayla that
I was going over to Miss Heather's house.*

*Kara and Kayla both said wow she invited you to
her house. Kara said are you going to fuck her if
she wants it. I said hell yeah, I'll fuck her if she
wants cock. Kayla said I bet her pussy is wet right
now waiting for you to come over. I said I hope
so. I hugged and kissed both Kayla and Kara.
Kayla said I think you need to slap both of our big
asses for good luck. They both bent over and lifted
up their summer dresses.*

*I smacked all four of their ass cheeks for good luck
and they both moaned with pleasure. I said oh
yeah, I'm ready now. I climbed into my Toyota
Tundra and drove to Miss Heather's house. I*

*stopped on the way and got her some flowers as
Kayla suggested.*

*I got a dozen roses for my Miss Heather. I rang
her doorbell. Miss Heather opened the door in the
sexiest red dress ever. I said hello Miss Heather,
these are for you. She said hello to you too sweetie
come on in, she said thank you then put the flowers
down and hugged me tight. She said thanks for
coming over and I said very happy to be here.*

*She took my hand leading me to her living room.
Dinner was on the table, and it was like 5 different
types of pasta. It looked and smelt delicious. We
sat down smiling then we dug into the pasta. It
was delicious and I told Miss Heather so. She said
thank you, I'm glad you like it. We ate until we
were both full. Miss Heather put the rest away.
We did the dishes together smiling the whole time
looking at each other.*

*After the dishes, she said you can stop calling me
Miss Heather you are no longer my student. I said
very well then Heather. She took my hand, and we
went to her couch. We sat down facing each other,
both nervous as hell. Heather leaned in and kissed*

me. I held her tight and kissed her right back. We made out for a long time.

All our nervousness went away, and Heather said let's go to my bedroom. It's more comfortable there, I said sure Heather lead the way. She took my hand and we walked to her bedroom. It was filled with vanilla scented candles, it smelt incredible with amazing ambience.

Heather stood before me and took off all of my clothes. I was at full attention, and she said I love your big black cock. I took her dress off, I undid her bra then I took her panties off.

Heather knelt before me and swallowed my cock with expert skill over and over. It was the best blow job ever then she stopped crawled on the bed. I crawled between her legs and kissed her sweet white thighs. I blew on her shaved white pussy. I licked up and down her delicious pink slit.

I inserted my middle finger into her pussy. Heather said wow long fingers that's when I started sucking on her clit. She held my head as I applied more pressure and suction to her clit until Heather floated on cloud nine. I said its time, I said are you ready Heather. She said I hope so you're really big baby.

I forged my way into Heather's pussy roughly. I squeezed her big tits and fucked her hard. Heather screamed with pleasure as I fucked her harder and harder. We both saw her creaming my cock over and over. I bent her over and fucked her hard. I smack her big ass hard and pulled her hair. Heather really liked it by lubricated my cock again.

Heather told me to lie down baby. I laid down and Heather held my hard-black cock and slid her white pussy down my black pole. I squeezed her big fucking titties and nipples as she fucked me hard. I moaned oh Heather, you are the sexiest teacher as I ejaculated everything in my balls into my Heather.

Heather leaned down and kissed me. We held each other tight in total silence for a while until Heather rolled off me. She held my hands and said I've fantasized about this for so long, it was incredible. I said I agree with you, my Heather. She smiled and held my face. I said I'm glad our feelings are mutual Heather. She said I'm happy about that too, my favorite student.

We went to sleep after I texted Kayla and Kara that I was spending the night with Heather. I woke up to Heather's pretty face. She said good morning my new lover and I said good morning my Heather. She smiled and said I love being your Heather. She said do you want to shower with me. I said hell yeah. We climbed in the shower and turned it on.

Heather said you soap me up and then I'll soap you up honey. I took my time and soaped up all of Heathers delicious goodies. She smiled the whole time and so did I. After I was done, she said my turn. She soaped up my hard cock then the rest of me.

Heather bent over and said stick your big dick in me, don't stop until you cum. I said yes, my Heather. I slammed my cock up her cunt and pounded Heather without mercy. She screamed bloody murder as I fucked her hard. I lost track of how many times she came on my cock. I gave it to her until my balls tingled, and I released all my warm sperm into her vagina.

Heather said oh my god so good I've never lost track of orgasm's before, thank you sweetheart. I said no thank you my vanilla goddess. We exited the shower and took turns drying each other off. We ate breakfast thoroughly satisfied and happy. We were smiling the whole time in our robes.

When we were done with breakfast. I put my clothes back on and got ready to go home. We hugged and kissed goodbye. I went home Sunday morning to Kara and Kayla. Both said the walk of shame. I smiled and I said it was worth it to thoroughly satisfy every inch of Heather's delicious body.

A few days later, I walked into the kitchen and Kayla was bent over in the fridge. I could see her pussy which gave me an instant boner. I took my boxers off and slammed my hard cock up her bare cunt. I started pumping and Kayla started moaning oh honey you haven't forgotten your white mommy. I said I'll never forget your sweet white pussy and she said I'll never forget your big pleasure stick.

Kayla moaned oh god I love your big ass black cock so good to your white mommy's pussy. I saw her pussy cream coating my black cock deep in her white pussy. It really turns me on every time she creams my cock. We both heard Kara said wow that is the best watching my white mommy take a huge black cock in her white pussy.

I said your white mommy's pussy is pretty great. Kara said don't clean your cock, when your done with my mother. I want you to fuck me with your dirty cock, cream and all. I said oh god yes, ejaculating my sperm into Kayla's tight little pussy.

I smacked her juicy ass and pulled out of her cunt. She turned around and said that was great honey before kissing me passionately in front of her daughter. Kayla and I held each other for a while. I looked back and Kara was gone. I said I better go find her.

I went to go look for Kara. She was waiting by my door totally naked. I said hey sexy want some black in you. Kara said oh yeah, I want the same treatment you gave my mother on prom night. I said my pleasure. I kissed her passionately and we fell against the wall. Kara spread her legs and my hard cock slid between her sweet white thighs. I could feel her wetness. Kara was ready for cock as she jumped on my hips.

I held her thighs and lowered her down my black pole. I fucked her hard as I kissed her neck and she kissed mine. She moaned I love your big fucking cock so good to my pussy as she creamed my cock and balls. I said assume the position sweet cheeks. I smacked her juicy ass and then penetrated her white pussy deep with my black cock. I fucked the shit out of her pussy from behind holding her hips firm so she wouldn't try to get away.

I said damn Kara so good as I ejaculated into her white vagina. She kissed me passionately and we both heard Kayla say wow that was steamy as hell. We both looked at Kayla smiling, Kara said I hope Heather doesn't mind us giving you some white pussy when she isn't around. I said I hope not.

A month later, Kayla and Kara suggested that I invite Heather over for dinner since I've been banging her like a drum for a month. I said sure I'll asked her. Heather said sure no problem. The night of the dinner. Heather showed up looking incredible in a revealing little black dress barely holding her dangerous curves.

Kayla, Kara and I greeted Heather at the door. I hugged, kissed and felt up Heather sexy big ass welcoming her to our home. Kayla said welcome hugging and kissing Heather on the lips. Heather didn't overreact so Kara hugged and kissed her too.

I said dinner is ready shall we eat. We sat down to eat pasta, and everyone was all smiles. We all talked like normal to my surprise. We all gave up when we were full. I said come Heather let me show you, my bedroom. Kayla and Kara said see you guys later.

Heather and I were in my room hanging out holding hands when we heard screaming. We both looked out my bedroom window. Kayla and Kara were in the pool splashing each other naked. I said oh god they are naked, I can see their big ass titties. Heather said oh wow your huge cock is hard as shit, that's so kinky, are you turned on by their big tits.

I said yeah, I'm sorry Heather. She said no I like kinky. I said you do and she said you want to go outside naked and surprise them. I said hell yeah, you are the coolest girlfriend ever. Heather smiled turning red. We took all our clothes off and went out to the pool. Kayla and Kara were too busy splashing each other to notice we were there naked too.

Heather said hey naked girls really loud. They turned around and said oh my god you guys are here. Kayla said wow that's big fucking cock and Kara wow that is a really big black cock. Heather said, oh yes, it is, stroking my black cock then she surprised me by getting on her knees.

She started sucking my cock then deep throating my cock with Kayla and Kara watching with happy faces. Kayla chanted suck that dick and Kara chanted suck that dick for a while until I was overwhelmed with pleasure. I ejaculated my warm

The end